W9-CSR-428

The Berenstain Bears
AND TOO MUCH
PRESSURE

When cubs and their parents
get a little too busy,
their everyday lives
get a little too dizzy.

A First Time Book®

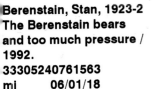

The Berenstain Bears AND TOO MUCH PRESSURE

Stan & Jan Berenstain

Random House 🏠 New York

Copyright © 1992 by Berenstain Enterprises, Inc. All rights reserved.
Published in the United States by Random House Children's Books,
a division of Random House, Inc., New York.
Random House and the colophon are registered trademarks of Random House, Inc.
First Time Books and the colophon are registered trademarks of Berenstain Enterprises, Inc.
randomhouse.com/kids   BerenstainBears.com
Library of Congress Cataloging-in-Publication Data
Berenstain, Stan. The Berenstain bears and too much pressure / Stan & Jan Berenstain.
p. cm. — (A First time book)
Summary: Members of the Bear family commit themselves to so many time-consuming activities
that the resulting stress brings on a crisis and makes them admit
that there are only so many hours in a day.
ISBN 978-0-679-83671-1 (trade) [1. Time—Fiction. 2. Stress (Psychology)—Fiction.
3. Bears—Fiction.] I. Berenstain, Jan. II. Title. III. Series: Berenstain, Stan. First time books.
PZ7.B4483Belt 1992 [E]—dc20 92-06544
Printed in the United States of America   36 35 34 33 32 31 30 29 28 27 26 25

If someone were to ask you who Bear Country's busiest creatures are, you might answer that bees are the busiest. They gather nectar and pollen, make honey, guard the hive, and do all the other things that have earned them the title Busy Bees.

Or you might answer that beavers are the busiest. They fell trees, make dams, and build lodges with secret underwater entrances. There's no question about it, beavers certainly are busy.

But if you were to answer bees or beavers, you would be wrong. Because the busiest creatures in Bear Country, lately, are none other than our friends the Bear family.

The Bears haven't always been so busy. They used to do the things that most families do: they worked and played, went to school, visited friends, enjoyed nature—and once in a while they just sat around and did absolutely nothing.

The Bears hadn't planned on becoming so busy—it sort of sneaked up on them. First, there was Brother Bear and the Little League.

Then, Sister Bear got bitten by the ballet bug and started ballet class.

When her best friend, Lizzy Bruin, started riding lessons, Sister just *had* to take that up too—and Brother wasn't about to be left out of something as exciting as horseback riding.

That's how it was with other activities. As soon as one of the cubs' friends signed up for something, Brother and Sister had to sign up too. Before anyone thought to say enough is enough, they were also signed up for...

swimming,

gymnastics,

soccer,

SOCCER IS HOW WE GET OUR KICKS!

Talk about busy! Mama or Papa Bear had to *drive* Brother and Sister to all those activities!

Things got so complicated that Mama had to make a big schedule to keep things straight. Papa hung it on the wall.

The schedule was especially difficult on Friday—and today was Friday.

"Will somebody answer the phone?" called Mama, after the fourth ring. "I'm busy getting things out of the freezer for tonight's dinner."

"Can't right now!" shouted Sister from upstairs. "I'm getting ready for ballet!"

"Me neither!" yelled Brother. "I'm getting on my baseball stuff!"

Since Papa was out working on the car, Mama had to answer the phone. She reached it by the seventh ring. It seemed a lot longer to Gran on the other end.

"Hello?" said Mama.

"Hello, dear," said Gran. "Is everything all right? You sound a little breathless."

"Just a little," said Mama. "I was in the kitchen getting dinner out of the freezer. The cubs are upstairs getting dressed for ballet and baseball, and Papa—"

But before she could explain about Papa, her shoulder bag got tangled in the phone cord, which pulled the phone down with a clunk.

"What happened?" shouted Gran. "There was an awful clunk!"

CLUNK!

"It was just the phone falling—was there anything special, Gran?" What Mama didn't explain was that when she stooped to pick up the phone, her hat fell off, and when she reached for it, she tripped over the cord and was now sitting in a tangled heap on the floor.

"I was just calling to invite you all to dinner sometime soon," said Gran.

"Love to, Gran. But we're just on our way out, so let me check our schedule and get back to you."

"Fine," Gran said after a pause. "Well, g'bye."

"Mama!" said Sister. "What are you doing sitting on the floor playing with the phone cord? C'mon, we're going to be late!"

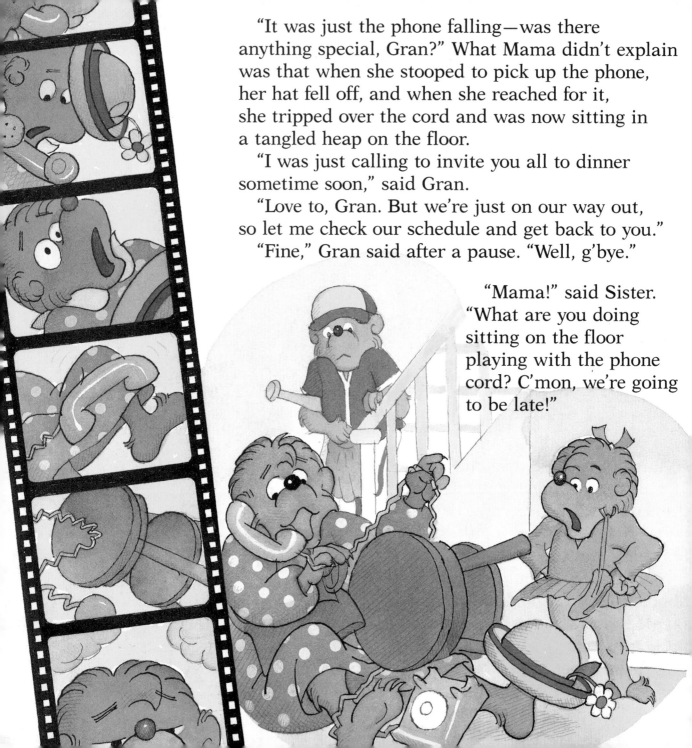

"Drop me off first!" shouted Brother on the way to the car.

"No! Me first!" cried Sister.

"No, me!" insisted Brother.

When Papa tried to explain what had been wrong with the car—the spark plugs needed cleaning—Mama shouted, "Not now, dear!" and roared off, leaving him in a cloud of dust.

"Well," Gran said as she hung up the phone, "there certainly is a lot going on over at the tree house."

"That's the way young folks are," said Gramps. "They like to get out and *do* things. Why, when I was a young feller—"

"*Doing* is one thing," said Gran. "*Over*doing," she added with a sigh, "is something else again."

If Papa could have heard Gran, he surely would have agreed. There was too much going on—too much coming and going, too much rushing about, *too much pressure.* The Bear family's schedule was becoming a nightmare— as it turned out, a whole series of nightmares.

The cubs had planned to watch some TV that evening, but they were so stiff and tired—Sister from ballet, Brother from baseball—that they went to bed early, fell asleep, and dreamed.

Sister dreamed she was on a strange sort of merry-go-round— a merry-go-round of activities, which went round and round and round. She wanted to get off, but no matter how hard she tried, she couldn't.

Brother had a dream too. He dreamed he was caught up in an enormous whirlwind of baseballs, soccer balls, and computers.

Papa dreamed he was trapped on a magic carpet that was zooming into a deep black hole. Only it wasn't a magic carpet. It was that awful schedule from the wall.

Mama didn't have a nightmare. The reason was that she didn't fall asleep all night. She lay awake staring into the darkness, wondering how she was going to get through the next day.

After a quick breakfast, Mama packed
a lunch for Papa, who headed for some
work in the forest. Then she shooed the
cubs into the car. "Hurry!" she said.
"We have a difficult day ahead of us.
There's art class, soccer, karate, and
swimming, and we've got to squeeze in
lunch and shopping!"

They climbed into the car, and she turned the key. But the engine wouldn't start. She tried again, but it still wouldn't start.

"Please, Mama!" shouted Brother. "Our karate instructor is very strict about being late!"

"And the soccer coach is worse!" yelled Sister.

Mama tried again and again.

"Please, Mama!" they screamed, jumping up and down in the back seat. But no matter how hard she tried, the car just would not start.

Then Mama did something the cubs had
never seen her do before. She started
to cry. Big wet tears rolled down her
cheeks. The cubs forgot karate and
soccer and everything else except
that their mama was crying.

"What's the matter?" asked Brother.

"Tell us, *please!*" begged Sister.
But Mama just went boohooing up
the front steps and into the house.

"Go get Papa!" Sister said to
Brother. "I'll stay with Mama."

Sister followed Mama up to her room, where she fell on the bed sobbing. It was all Sister could do to keep from crying herself.

"It's Mama! You gotta come!" shouted Brother as he reached Papa's workplace in the woods. He told Papa what happened. Papa could see that he was upset about Mama crying.

"Everybody cries once in a while, Son," he said.

"Even you?" asked Brother.

"Sometimes," Papa said. "The problem with the car is those spark plugs. We probably need new ones. But the real problem is this schedule of ours. I know Mama didn't sleep well last night worrying about it."

"I didn't sleep too well, either. I had this awful dream," admitted Brother.

"That makes two of us," said Papa.

"Sister had one too," said Brother as they reached the tree house.

"Mama stopped crying!" announced Sister as Papa and Brother came upstairs.

"That's right," Mama said, smiling through a few last tears. "There's nothing like a good cry sometimes."

"And there's nothing like a little common sense about too much pressure," said Papa.

So the bears had a family meeting right then and there. The cubs agreed that two after-school activities a week were more than enough. Brother chose baseball and computer club. Sister chose ballet and horseback riding.

True—they lost their title The Busiest Family in Bear Country. But they went back to having a very good time doing the everyday things that most families do. They worked and played, went to school, visited friends, enjoyed nature—

and once in a while, they sat
around doing absolutely
nothing.